DESMARAIS

W9-BMB-696

First edition for the United States
published 1993 by Barron's Educational Series, Inc.

First published 1993 by J.M. Dent, The Orion Publishing
Group, London, England

All inquiries should be addressed to:
Barron's Educational Series, Inc.
250 Wireless Boulevard
Hauppauge, New York 11788

Library of Congress Catalog Card No. 92-39671
International Standard Book No. 0-8120-5791-0 (hardcover)
0-8120-1552-5 (paperback)


Library of Congress Cataloging-in-Publication Data

Smith, Iris.
    Little witch/Iris Smith : illustrated by Caroline Church —
1st ed. for the U.S.
        p.  cm.
    Summary: Wiggy, who is still learning how to be a witch, loses her
way and her magic broomstick while collecting berries in the woods.
    ISBN 0-8120-5791-0. — ISBN 0-8120-1552-5 (pbk.)
    [1. Witches — Fiction,  2. Lost children — Fiction.]  I. Church,
Caroline, ill.  II. Title.
PZ7.S6495L1  1993
[E] — dc20                                          92-39671
                                                     CIP
                                                      AC


PRINTED IN ITALY
3456            987654321

# Little Witch

Iris Smith
Illustrated by Caroline Church

BARRON'S

Once long ago when forests were full of magic and witches wove spells, there lived a little witch called Wiggy.

She was excited because she had received a new caldron on her birthday—not a full-sized one, but one big enough to mix some extra special spells in. Wiggy put some herbs into the caldron and sang:

"Shoes in cupboards, clothes on hooks.
Tidy up my toys and all my books."

Everything flew around the room. Her shoes hung themselves on hooks and her clothes piled themselves up on the floor. Oh, dear! Wiggy had got the spell all mixed up.

She threw some red flowers into the caldron.

"Spells are magic. Spells are fun.

Spell book find a special one," she chanted.

*The Second Book of Spells* jumped from the shelf, and fell open in front of her—upside down. She turned it around.

"A spell to make children fly," she read. Wiggy giggled mischievously. "Yes, that's the one I'll try first!"

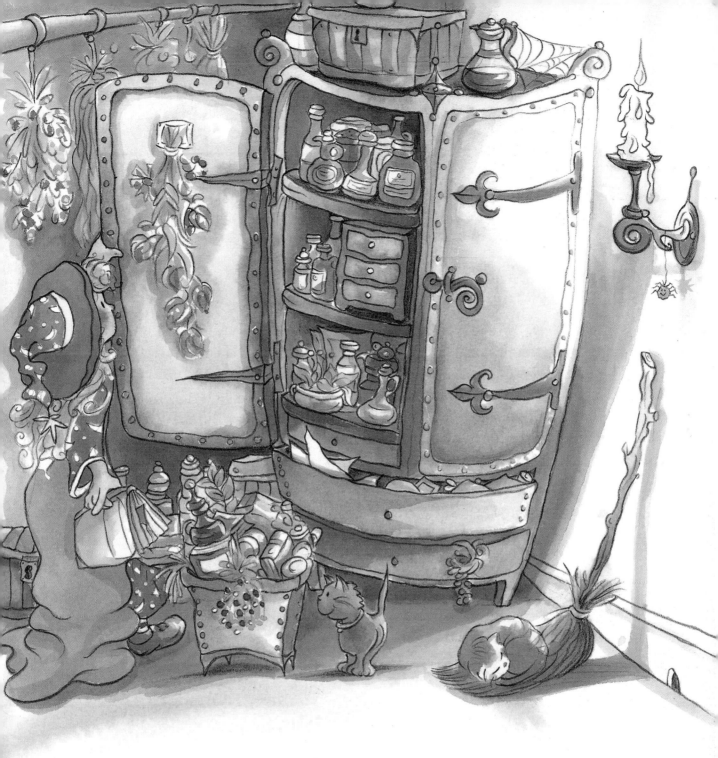

There was a long list of things to make the spell work. Most of them were in her mother's pantry, but Wiggy had to pick some fresh red, green, and blue berries.

"I'm going to collect some berries," she called.

"Don't go far," warned her mother, "and don't forget your broomstick."

Wiggy shook the sleepy cat off her broomstick and flew across the rooftops.

She did not stop to hear her mother's last words, which were: "Remember to put a spell on your broomstick or it will slip off and hide from you!"

Wiggy soon arrived at the woods. She dropped her
broomstick and started collecting berries right away.
She was so busy she did not see her broomstick dance
off between the trees.

She did not hear the breeze blow through the treetops and she did not notice the falling leaves cover the forest floor. When her basket was full, she turned to pick up the broomstick—but it was nowhere in sight.

"Broomstick mine, wherever you be,
   Leave that place and come to me," she called.
   But the broomstick did not come. Wiggy pushed
back her tall pointed hat and scratched her head. She
looked in despair at all the leaves on the ground.
However was she going to find her broomstick? She
kicked aside the nearest heap of leaves.

"Do you mind!" squeaked a hedgehog angrily.

"I'm sorry," cried Wiggy. "Please will you help me? I've lost my broomstick and I can't get home."

"I'm getting ready for winter. I'm much too busy," said the hedgehog, and he turned his back and disappeared under another pile of leaves.

"Broomstick, broomstick, do not roam.
   Come to me and take me home," wailed Wiggy, but
the broomstick did not come.
   "Do be quiet," grumbled an owl in the treetop.
"You're disturbing my sleep."
   "Please will you help me?" sobbed Wiggy. "I've lost
my broomstick and I can't get home."

"Then stay where you are. I'm much too tired." The owl closed his bright round eyes and went back to sleep.

Wiggy did not stay where she was. She looked behind trees and peered beneath bushes—her long black cloak flying behind her.

She climbed an old elm and looked down its hollow trunk, and she crawled into a foxhole.

She searched through the knotted stems of ivy and she got tangled up in the brambles. Still she could not find her broomstick.

"Oh, dear. Oh, dear," she sighed, and she sat down at the foot of an oak tree. She was completely lost.

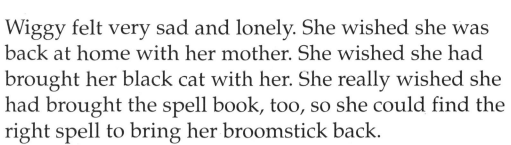

Wiggy felt very sad and lonely. She wished she was back at home with her mother. She wished she had brought her black cat with her. She really wished she had brought the spell book, too, so she could find the right spell to bring her broomstick back.

"Oh, dear. Oh, dear. Oh, dear," Wiggy cried again, and five huge tears rolled down her cheeks and dropped onto the ground.

The oak tree shook its branches angrily
and made its leaves rustle.

"Please don't do that," they seemed to whisper.

"Please will you help me?" asked Wiggy. "I've lost
my broomstick and I can't get home."

"We can't help. We're much too busy." The leaves
jumped from the tree and swirled and spun around
Wiggy until she felt dizzy.

The forest grew cold and dark. The moon rose and
spread patterns of pale light through the branches.

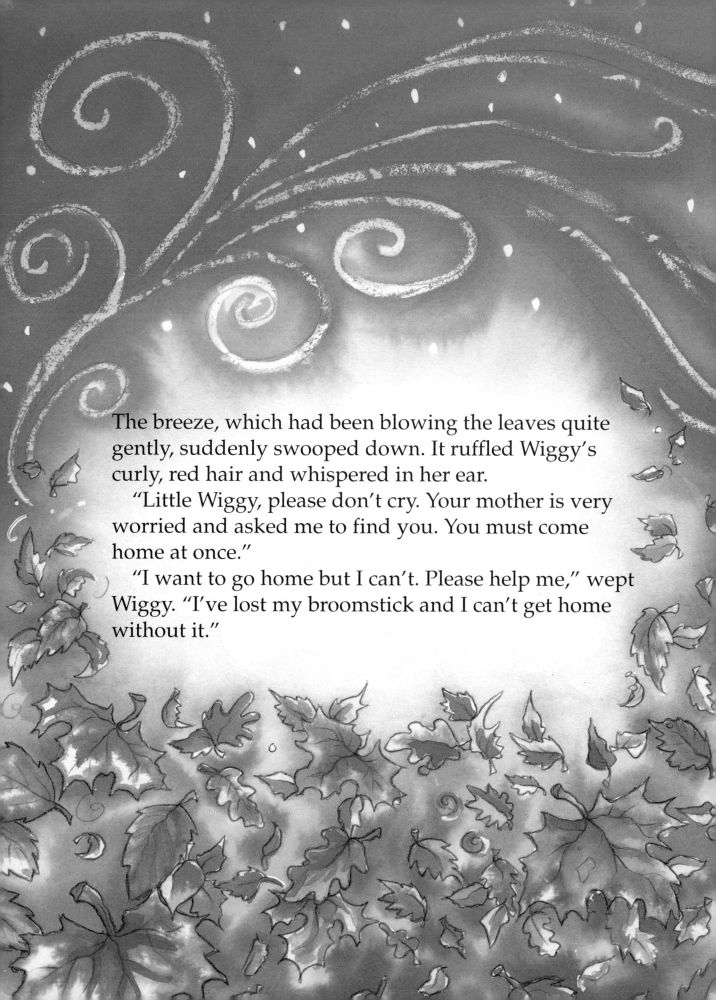

The breeze, which had been blowing the leaves quite gently, suddenly swooped down. It ruffled Wiggy's curly, red hair and whispered in her ear.

"Little Wiggy, please don't cry. Your mother is very worried and asked me to find you. You must come home at once."

"I want to go home but I can't. Please help me," wept Wiggy. "I've lost my broomstick and I can't get home without it."

The breeze took a big breath and changed from a
breeze into a wind. Then it took another big breath and
changed into a gale. Then it blew, and blew, and blew.
It blew so hard that the trees shook. The hedgehog buried
himself deeper in his bed. The owl held tight to his branch.
The oak tree trembled but stood firm.

 The leaves jumped up and danced. Around and around
they whirled, faster and faster, until they were
so tired they fell into heaps on the ground.

The wind blew harder still and swept all the leaves from a path in the middle of the forest. There, in a circle of yellow moonlight, lay the broomstick.

"Thank you, thank you!" cried Wiggy, and with a whoop of delight, she leapt on her broomstick. She waved good-bye to the forest and flew home as fast as she could.

The broomstick landed right outside her house and there, waiting on the doorstep, were Wiggy's mother and her black cat.

"Oh, Mommy," cried Wiggy, "I'm so glad to be home. I'll never do that again." Her mother gave Wiggy a hug. Then she took her hand and they went inside—followed by the cat and the broomstick. Outside, the breeze blew a soft tune before going quietly back to the forest.